JUST KICKIN' IT

JULIE THOMPSON

ORCA BOOK PUBLISHERS

Published in Canada and the United States
in 2025 by Orca Book Publishers.
orcabook.com

Library and Archives Canada Cataloguing in Publication
Title: Just kickin' it / Julie Thompson.
Other titles: Just kicking it
Names: Thompson, Julie, 1972- author.
Series: Orca anchor.
Description: Series statement: Orca anchor
Identifiers: Canadiana (print) 20240321499 | Canadiana (ebook) 20240323637 | ISBN 9781459841017 (softcover) | ISBN 9781459841031 (EPUB) | ISBN 9781459841024 (PDF)
Subjects: LCGFT: High interest-low vocabulary books. | LCGFT: Novels.
Classification: LCC PS8639.H62675 J87 2025 | DDC jC813/.6—dc23

Library of Congress Control Number: 2024933327

Summary: In this high-interest accessible novel for teen readers, sixteen-year-old Jesse wonders how far he'll go for a cool new pair of sneakers when an older teen entices him into petty theft.

Orca Book Publishers is committed to reducing the consumption of nonrenewable resources in the production of our books. We make every effort to use materials that support a sustainable future.

Orca Book Publishers gratefully acknowledges the support for its publishing programs provided by the following agencies: the Government of Canada, the Canada Council for the Arts and the Province of British Columbia through the BC Arts Council and the Book Publishing Tax Credit.

Design by Ella Collier.
Cover illustration by Getty Images/ilyailya.
Edited by Gabrielle Prendergast.
Author photo by Helen Tansy Photography.

Printed and bound in Canada.

28 27 26 25 • 1 2 3 4

To GG

Chapter One

Ding-dong!

I was staring at my empty money box when I heard the doorbell ring. Yesterday I had $250 in there. But this morning I woke up with no Wi-Fi. I asked my grandpa about it.

"We're a bit short of money lately," he said. "I let some bills slide."

Two months ago Grandpa's car broke down. He had to pay to get it fixed. That had messed things up, moneywise. And so the Wi-Fi was off. I can't live without Wi-Fi. I don't even have a data plan on my phone.

So I handed over my savings. All $250. Grandpa walked down to the bank to pay the bill. The Wi-Fi is back on now. But my money box is empty.

I sighed as I slid the box back under my bed.

"I'll get it, Grandpa," I said, taking the stairs two at a time. I felt my heart skip a beat. I put my hand on the doorknob. I pulled hard on the handle.

"What up, J?" Tay said.

"What you sayin', Tay?"

Facing each other, we began our special greeting. Left hand over right. Right finger snap. Two steps in. Left shoulder bump. Right shoulder bump. Two steps back. Head tilted to the left. Two-finger rub.

"Yo, crisp kicks!" I said.

Purple and orange Steps. Tay's newest kicks. He had over twenty-five pairs stored. In his "shoebox." Not an actual shoebox. It was a small closet beside his bedroom. His shoebox made my room look like a matchbox.

"How much?" I asked.

"Three and a half bills," Tay said, smiling. If you didn't know Tay, you might think he was being a jerk. But he wasn't. He was just real proud of his shoes.

Tay and I are best friends. But our lives are very different.

Tay's family has a lot of money. He gets a new pair of kicks every month. Me, on the other hand, I'm the kid standing outside the shoe store. Face pressed against the window. Dreaming and hoping.

That's what the $250 was supposed to be for. I had been saving for months.

Three years ago a new pair of kicks would have been no biggie. Life was good. I wasn't living life like Tay, mind you. Tay's family is next-level. But I had the best parents. A nice home. One minute I was a kid who was on top of the world. The next minute...

I was an orphan. My parents were killed on vacation. They were heading home from the airport. A semi crossed the line. My folks were pushed off the road. Down a hill into a ravine. The coroner said they were killed instantly.

I was staying with my grandpa when it happened. I will never forget. Two cops showed up at his place. They asked if they could come in. When cops show up at your door, asking to come in, the natural answer is "Hellz no." But something about these officers was different. They looked serious yet sad.

The female officer spoke to Grandpa first. "My name is Sergeant Joan Riley, and this is my partner, Constable Don Kingsley. We are sorry to tell you that your son and daughter-in-law were killed in a car accident. It happened earlier this morning."

I couldn't tell you what she said after that. My mind shut down. I was transported to a different place and time. All I remember is my grandpa's voice. Calling my name. His arms wrapped around me as he guided me to the couch. I had no idea, the day my folks dropped me off at my grandpa's, that I would be there forever. If I had, I might have hugged them a little harder. Or begged them not to go. But the past can't be changed.

My parents didn't know they were going to die. Most people don't. But they made plans. They had life insurance. My grandpa used some of that money to buy a little place close to where my parents and I used to live. They didn't own the house we'd lived in.

They'd rented it. They didn't want to be tied down to one spot.

Funny thing is, I'd lived in that house most of my life. My grandpa wanted to buy it. But I needed a fresh start. There were too many memories in that house. One good thing, I was able to stay in the neighborhood. Go to the same school. Still hang with my friends. Some of the money was used to pay for my parents' funeral. Whatever was left over was to live on.

My grandpa is retired, but he gets money every month. From the place he used to work at. But we can't seem to make it stretch. I have clean clothes and food. But truth be told, sometimes the food is not enough.

I get hungry. I try not to complain. I know my grandpa is doing his best.

That's why I'd saved for a pair of crisp kicks. Two hundred and fifty dollars. It took me close to a year. I did odd jobs here and there. Helping out folks in the neighborhood. Mowing lawns, shoveling snow. It wasn't a ton of money, but every little bit helped. I planned on getting a part-time job in September. That way I wouldn't have to wait a year to buy the things I want. Grandpa wanted me to keep all the money I'd made. But without Wi-Fi I have no life. No music. Hardly any friends. And I am going to do an online computer course this summer too. Just to get ahead a bit in school.

Eleventh grade feels like a big deal. I want to be a regular kid. I don't want to stand out.

I want to be just another sixteen-year-old with sick kicks. Just like my dad.

He collected shoes. Jordans. In fact, he wanted to name me Jordan. My mom wasn't having it. Her only son wasn't going to be named after a sneaker. They settled on Jesse. Stupid thing is, Dad had small feet. His shoes don't fit me.

I wanted to get my own pair. To give me street cred with my friends. And keep my dad close to me. And step out with Tay and look as fly as him.

Tay and I have been best friends since third grade. He showed up that September. The new kid at the school. Him and his older brother, Andrew. His father worked for a tech company. The company was growing, and they asked Tay's dad to open an office in Milson. When Tay arrived, Mr. Ross, our principal, asked me to show him how things are done at Baldwin Elementary. We hit it off from the start. And, like they say, the rest is history.

It's easy to like Tay. Always laughing. Not like the class clown. He just has the funniest jokes. Even makes the teachers laugh. I trust him with all my secrets. He's what you call a ride-or-die friend.

No matter what, we always have each other's backs.

I was busy admiring Tay's shoes. I didn't see my grandpa standing behind me.

"Where you boys off to?" Grandpa asked.

"We're going to meet up with some friends," I said.

"Nothing special," Tay said.

It was a nice day. I couldn't wait to get on my bike.

When the weather is nice, Tay and I ride our bikes all day. We leave first thing in the morning. Get back with the streetlights on.

"I'll be back in time for dinner," I said.

"Got your phone with you?" Grandpa asked.

"Yeah. It's in my pocket."

Even on our budget, Grandpa did get me a cell. Pay as you go. No data. I can text and make calls. And take photos or video—but I can't send them anywhere without Wi-Fi.

Wi-Fi. Ugh. My $250 down the tubes.

"Tay, you staying for dinner?" Grandpa asked.

"You couldn't stop me. Thanks, Mr. Clark!"

"Dinner at six. Don't be late," Grandpa said.

"We won't," I shouted as we rode off.

On a good day we ride for hours. When we're hungry, we stop at Star Burger for lunch. Or Mr. Yang's shop for drinks. All the kids hang out at Mr. Yang's. He is Korean. Doesn't look like half the people in our town. We hang out there because Mr. Yang treats us a bit better than the white shop owners.

The white stores only allow a few of us in at a time. Not all of them are like that. But enough that it makes us feel a way.

We're used to it. If you are a Black kid, you are treated differently. In the stores. By the cops. On TV. And at school. The media spreads fear. The world believes the lies. Especially when it comes to Black boys. The media should just do us a favor and put their true feelings on blast. If they did, the headline would read *BLACK BOYS CAN'T BE TRUSTED.*

My parents told me some crazy stories about things that had happened to them. And it seems like nothing much has changed.

I wouldn't say Mr. Yang is racist, but he has a little hate on for all the kids. Regardless of their skin color. But today the store would be rammed. So Mr. Yang would do what he always did. Yell at us to "get what you need and go!" Yang's store has everything. And it is easy to get to. That's why all the kids hang out there. So Tay and I stopped to get a soda. It was summer. The weather was hot.

"You buying, J?" Tay asked.

"Nah, son," I said. "You dropped three and a half bills on kicks. You can spot me." I didn't want to tell him about the Wi-Fi bill. Or my empty money box.

"Facts. I got you," Tay said as he smiled.

I thought about that as he walked ahead of me into the store. He wasn't lying. He always had my back.

Chapter Two

The slushy machine was working hard. It was like all the kids from the town were in the store.

I remember how nice some of the kids were when my folks died. Their parents too. They brought us food. They called it a food train. I remember my folks used to watch *Soul Train*. But until they died, I had never heard of a train that brought food.

I wouldn't mind the food train rolling through again. I don't think I'll get any taller, but I'm still filling out. And a growing boy needs a lot of food.

Yeah, part of the town is real wack. I could do without the racism and Yang's yelling. But when my family needed help, good folks came together.

Tay paid for our drinks. We stopped to talk with a few friends. Then out the door we went, heading for the waterfront.

Tay was going to meet up with some guy he met last year on vacation. Some brother named Derick. Tay called him D for short. He was three years older than us. I wasn't happy about it. I was a little jealous. The summer was for us. Not some third wheel.

Tay said he was cool. So I was down for a meet and greet. But nothing more. It took fifteen minutes to get to the waterfront.

"Where your boy at?" I asked Tay.

"He'll be here soon," Tay said. "Chill. We're early."

We locked up our bikes and headed toward the water.

After my parents died, I spent a lot of time at the waterfront. The water was calming. I felt at peace. The waves helped me get out of my head.

But there still were some tough days. Days I spent crying. On those days, this place helped a lot. I would put my feet in the cold water. And let the tears drip right into the lake.

This place always reminded me of my dad.

When I was here, I felt like I could hear his voice.

His words of wisdom.

It's not what you have, it's what you make of it.

Sometimes you need to do what scares you most.

It's only impossible if you think it is.

Solid words from a solid man.

My daydreaming was cut short.

"Tay!!"

Tay turned toward the parking lot. There was a dude sitting on the hood of a white Mustang convertible. He was waving at Tay.

"Who's that?" I asked.

"That's my boy Derick," Tay said. "Goes by D."

My mouth dropped. This was no boy! Derick had a full goatee.

He also had a good thirty pounds on each of us. And his wheels! None of the kids we hung with had a car. Not even Tay's brother, and his family was loaded.

"Yo, why didn't you tell me your boy had wheels?" I whispered.

"Tssh, no biggie," Tay said. "Just chill, yo."

First, it was too hot outside to *chill*. Second, D was flexing in a shiny new Mustang. It was a big deal.

"Just be cool, bro." Tay elbowed me. "We don't want him to think we're soft."

"Ya, ya, I hear you. I'm good, bro. I'm good," I said. But inside something kinda felt off.

I followed behind Tay, acting as chill as I could.

"Yo, bro, what's up?" Tay said.

The two hugged.

"Not much. I'll be around all summer," Derick said. "Hanging out with my boys. Got a new hot ride."

Ain't that the truth, I said to myself.

"Yo, your ride is fresh," I said.

Derick didn't seem to notice me. It gave me a few seconds to give him the once-over. Fresh ride. Fresh gear. Fresh cut.

And of course. Badass fresh kicks!!!

"Yo, you good?" Tay asked.

"Yeah, man, I'm good. Jesse," I said. I held out my fist.

"Derick. You can call me D," Derick said.

We didn't do the man hug. But I did get a fist bump.

"Nice kicks, man." That's what my mouth said. But what my mind said was something different. The story in my mind went something like this.

How the mother-father can you afford all this? I saved months for new kicks. And still didn't have enough.

Derick gave me a smirk. "Thanks, man."

"Jesse's been saving for a pair," Tay said.

"Oh yeah? How long?" Derick asked.

"A while," I said. Obviously I didn't want to talk about it.

"That's too bad," Derick said.

How could it be too bad?

"What if I told you that you could have a pair just like these by next week?" Derick asked.

Next week? Derick's kicks were nicer than Tay's. That meant more money.

"What do you mean?" I asked.

"Like I said. You could have money for a pair by next week." Derick grinned at me. "You wanna know how?" he asked.

Something didn't feel right.

But I really wanted the shoes. I really wanted a full money box again. Plus, what could go wrong? *No harm in listening to the man talk. Right?* Little did I know.

I would end up kickin' myself.

Chapter Three

The look on my face probably said it all. I knew Derick had money. Maybe even more money than Tay.

But in a week? Something inside of me was shouting, *No!* But I wanted them so bad.

"So you wanna hear or what?" Derick asked.

"Yeah, man, 'course!" I said, trying to play it cool.

"It's simple," Derick said. "Your boy Tay told me about Mr. Yang. How he treats you guys bad and everything."

Mr. Yang wasn't that bad, I thought, minus the yelling and following us around the store. "What about him?" I asked.

"Well, your boy said Mr. Yang is a bit of a jerk," Derick said. "A rich jerk."

Tay nodded. But he wasn't looking at me.

"Summertime, Yang's store is bumpin'," Derick went on. "More people means more money. More money means new kicks for you. We work as a team. You'll go in, let the old man follow you. Keep him away from the till. While you're being spinned, I'll grab the cash." Derick laughed. His eyes looked cold. "Swoop and scoop," he said.

I looked over at Tay again. He wasn't laughing, and he didn't seem fazed.

"How old is Mr. Yang?" Derick asked. He was all business again.

"How would I know?" I said.

"I bet he's at least seventy," Derick said.

My head was spinning. I got that Mr. Yang could be a jerk, but *robbing* the guy? And Tay seemed to be down with it. But why? Tay could buy anything he wanted! Plus, Mr. Yang treated him the best out of all of us. Probably because Tay came from money.

"Listen, no one is going to get hurt," Tay said.

"Trust me," Derick said.

I couldn't believe what I was hearing. "But—" I started.

"But what? I know how much you want new kicks," Tay said. "Derick said you could be part of it too. Mr. Yang won't even miss the money. If it's a no-go, no biggie. What do you want to do?"

What I wanted was to go home. Start my day over. Pretend like I'd never heard of the plan. Pretend my best friend hadn't lost his mind. Pretend like I'd never met Derick. Or D. Or D Nice Kicks. Whatever the hell his name was.

I had a better name for him. D Dumbass. This whole plan was stupid. But why was I considering it? What if we got caught? *But they did promise no one would get hurt...*

I thought of my empty money box again.

Before I knew it, the words came out of my mouth.

"I'm down."

Chapter Four

The bike ride home was hard. Tay didn't say a word. Even though we rode side by side. It felt like we were worlds apart.

We were coming up to Mr. Yang's shop. The streetlights were just coming on. The shop was still open.

My stomach started to turn. I knew it was trying to talk to me.

I felt like I had to throw up. I took a breath as we drove by the shop.

I turned to Tay. "I don't know why I said I would do it."

"I don't know why either," Tay said. "You don't have to do it."

I wished my parents were still alive. My dad would know what to do. I took a deep breath. Tried to hear his voice. Nothing.

"I said yes because I just want to be a normal kid. I want to be like you. You have everything! And if you don't have it, you can get it." I felt my heart beating faster. "You don't know how lucky you are, Tay." My voice began to get louder. I could feel my eyes starting to water.

When your parents die, crying comes easily.

"Your parents are alive, Tay!" Now I was shouting. "I will never see my parents again!"

Tay stopped. He looked at me as he got off his bike. Now it seemed like he was going to cry.

"I did this for you," he said. "I can get almost anything I want. Shoes, clothes, anything. But I know you can't. How many times have I said I would buy you a pair of shoes?"

I wanted him to shut up. "I don't know!" I shouted.

"Three? Four? Ten?" Tay said. "I said I would buy you a pair of shoes ten times. Each time you said no."

He was right. Each time I'd said no. I was tired of handouts. Tired of people feeling sorry for us. I wanted to show I could do it on my own.

I'm proud of you, son. I know you'll do what's right.

There was Dad's voice at last. But he was saying the wrong things.

The tears in my eyes began to dry. I was angry with Tay. But in an odd way, I did believe he was trying to look out for me. Now I wished I would have let him buy me the shoes.

We were off our bikes, walking them along a muddy part of the road. "But why Yang's shop?" I asked.

Tay sighed. "I didn't plan it that way. Derick said he was planning to spend the summer here. We got to talking about stuff."

"What kind of stuff?" I asked.

"We weren't talking about you," Tay said. "Well, at least not at the start. We were talking about shoes. Clothes, stuff like that. I told him you were saving for shoes. He said he had a plan that could help you get your shoes. He's done this before. He's never gotten caught. That's how he gets his money. That's how he gets all his stuff."

I stopped walking. "Is that how he got his car?" I asked.

"Some of it. Not the whole thing." Tay laughed. "But his clothes and shoes. No one's ever got hurt."

"How do you know?"

"Because he told me," Tay said. "Plus, you're my boy. I am not going to let anything bad happen to you." Tay leaned over and gave me one of the bro hugs. The same hug he gave Derick. “You trust me, right?” he asked.

I didn’t trust the plan. Or Derick. But I did trust Tay. “Yeah, I trust you,” I said.

How could I not? I’d known this guy since third grade. My ride or die.

“Listen, I’m starving,” Tay said. “Plus, your gramps will have words for us if we’re late for dinner.”

He wasn’t wrong. If my grandpa said dinner was at six, you’d better be there by five fifty-five. And I was starving too.

We got back on our bikes. Heading for home.

The air had cooled. Tay had my back. I had nothing to worry about.

Chapter Five

Days passed and suddenly it was Tuesday. Grandpa wasn't home. Tuesdays, he volunteered to drive cancer patients to their chemo treatments.

Alone, I had time to think. Tay and I were going to meet up with Derick today. To go over the plan. To make sure everyone knew what they had to do.

It was 10:00 a.m. That gave me time to get out of my head. I reached under my bed.

The silver box was cold. I pulled it out.

Placing it on my bed, I opened the lid.

Empty.

I was hoping there would be $250.

I was hoping for a miracle.

I slid it back under my bed.

Maybe a shower would help. Or maybe a bite to eat. I grabbed my towel. My legs felt heavy. My stomach began to grumble. I hadn't eaten much the night before.

The water bounced off my head. I could have stayed in the shower for hours.

But water costs money. Warm water costs more money. And warm long showers cost even more money.

I turned off the water. Slid the curtain open. Grabbed my towel and wrapped it around my body. I wiped the water from the mirror.

Tay had said Mr. Yang wouldn't get hurt. I trusted Tay. I was going to do this. I looked into my eyes. "You can do this, Jesse," I said. "New kicks. New you."

I was all in. I had no other choice. I had to stop thinking about it.

There was one thing for sure.

I wasn't going to let anyone know I was broke. I walked to my room and got dressed.

I looked at the clock. Eleven thirty. Where had the time gone? Too much time in my head. I only had fifteen minutes to eat breakfast.

I had to meet up with Derick and Tay at noon. We were meeting at the school. Tay had sent me a message.

Derick had wanted to pick me up. But I didn't want him near my home. I stuffed the toast into my mouth. Headed out the front door. I turned to lock it.

"Yo, man, you good?"

I looked back and saw Derick's car. Derick was in the driver's seat. Tay sat in the back. I was surprised. Pissed, actually. I had told Tay I'd meet them at the school. I didn't want this clown to know where I lived.

Derick smiled. Not a happy-to-see-you smile. More like a gotcha smile. Classic jerk move.

"What are you guys doing here?" I asked. "I thought we were going to meet at the school."

"Yeah, Tay told me," Derick said. "We boys now. I can't let my boy walk."

"I wasn't going to," I said. "I was going to ride my bike."

Derick laughed. "Nah, son. No way."

He tapped the seat beside him. "Get in."

I opened the door slowly. On any other day, I would be all in. But today was different. The Mustang didn't feel so cool.

I slid into the seat. I didn't want to be with Derick. I didn't trust him. But the car was so fresh. Derick pulled out of my driveway. He headed toward the school. As we drove through town, we got lots of stares.

Older kids. Younger kids. Adults. Everyone was looking at us.

I felt famous. Like I mattered. It sucks what money can do.

Derick had money. People probably thought he was important. Thought he was nice. But if they only knew the truth.

I stayed quiet for most of the ride, lost in my thoughts. I forgot what we were planning to do. But when I opened my eyes, everything came back.

Derick parked behind the school, facing a park. There were people out walking. Enjoying the day. I'm sure they weren't planning a robbery. I wished I was in their shoes.

Derick looked at me. "You sure you're

good, li'l man?" he asked. "Tay told me about the talk."

"The talk?" I asked, surprised.

"The talk you had on the way home last night. He said you still weren't sure. Maybe I can help you out. You see, I'm like, a businessman. If I want something, I make a plan and get it. I want kicks. I make a plan, and I get them. I want fresh clothes. I make a plan, and I get them. I wanted this car. I made a plan, and I got it." Derick was sure of himself. "We work as a team. We split what we get."

"Three ways?" I asked.

Derick pulled down his sunglasses. He looked at Tay and chuckled.

"No," Derick said, looking back at me. "It was my plan. We will be using my car. I am taking most of the risks. Only fair I should get more money. Half. You and Tay will split the other half. But don't worry, bro. If we don't get enough, I'll help you out."

I looked down at my feet. Same old shoes. I looked over at Derick. Fresh kicks. Different pair from yesterday. It didn't seem fair.

It's crazy, I know, but sometimes I wish my dad hadn't been a sneaker head. If he hadn't been, I probably wouldn't be in this situation.

Getting these kicks was bigger than just fitting in.

I knew it was wrong. But in my head, it felt like the shoes were the most important thing in the world.

"So what's the plan?" I asked.

Tay jumped in. "You go in. Yang's going

to follow you around the store. Get him away from the register. I grab the cash."

"What if there are people in the store?" I asked. "What about the cameras?"

"Yang's camera by the cash is a dud," Tay said.

"We'll be good," Derick piped in.

"What if Yang doesn't follow me?" I asked.

"You're Black," Derick said. "Yang ain't gonna let you leave his sight."

"We'll come in and split up," Tay said.

"Look, he can't follow *three* brothers at once. Give him a reason to follow you," Derick said.

"So when we planning on doing this?" I asked.

"Tonight," Derick said.

Chapter Six

As soon as I got out of Derick's car at my house, Tay jumped into the front seat.

"Pick you up at eight," he called out the car window.

Then they drove away.

I slowly made my way inside the house. I warmed up my food. But I spent most of my time playing with it. I knew I had to eat.

I didn't want to pass out. Well, maybe if I passed out. I wouldn't have to go, I thought. I shoved some bites into my mouth. But the food was tasteless. I threw the rest out. I felt bad. Money was tight. And here I was throwing away perfectly good food. I should have saved it.

Anyway, there was a good chance of me throwing up tonight.

Wouldn't it be funny if I threw up in Derick's car? All over his leather seats. A smile came over my face. It didn't last. Just a few seconds. Enough to take me away from the nightmare. I looked at the clock. I had a few hours before Derick and Tay would be back. I put my plate in the sink. Drank a glass of water. And headed to my room. I threw myself on my bed and closed my eyes. I was tired.

I took my phone out of my pocket and set it on my nightstand. I thought about setting the alarm. But I knew there was no way I would fall asleep.

I closed my eyes for a minute. Or at least it felt like it.

The next thing I knew, I was waking up to my phone ringing.

I sat straight up. My head began to throb.

"Hello," I said, as I rubbed my head.

"Yo, man, where you at?" It was Tay on the phone. He wasn't happy.

"Chill. I'm home. What's up? When you comin'?" I asked.

"When we comin'? We *been* here," Tay said.

I checked my phone. It was 8:15. I *did* fall asleep.

"Yo, tell your boy to get his ass out here right now!" Derick sounded annoyed. Angry. I could hear it in his voice.

"I'm coming," I said, throwing the covers off me. I changed into a darker shirt. They do that in the movies. I figured it wouldn't hurt.

Derick had parked his car in front of my house. Derick and Tay were both wearing dark shirts. Looked like we watched the same movies.

I got into the seat behind Tay.

"I'm sorry. I fell asleep," I said.

"You're lucky," Derick said. "I know it's your first time. You're nervous. But I've done this a hundred times. And guess how many people have gotten hurt?"

Before I could answer, Derick answered for me.

"None! Not one person," he said. "That's why I know it's gonna work out, li'l man. Trust me."

Trust? That's what got me into this. I swore I was going to punch the next person who said "trust me."

The air was cooler than usual. I rested my head on the seat. The breeze helped to relax me a bit as we drove by Mr. Yang's shop. It wasn't very busy. Just a few customers. Derick parked half a block away.

"So," he said to Tay. "If we're going to get this done, everyone has to be good." He wanted to make sure Tay wasn't mad at me for falling asleep. There couldn't be any beef between us.

Tay looked at Derick. "Yeah, we good," Tay said.

"Shake on it," Derick said.

Tay turned around. He stuck out his hand.

"We good," I said as we shook hands.

Derick seemed proud. Like he had done something great.

I wasn't stupid. Tay was doing this because of Derick. He wanted to do good by Derick. Either way Tay had been there for me so many times. It didn't really matter why he was doing it. I was just glad he was here with me.

"Okay, let's do this," Derick said.

I'd started to open the car door when I heard Derick's voice. "Oh yeah, li'l man, take this, just in case."

In his hand was a six-inch carving knife. I couldn't swallow.

"Take it," Derick said. "Just in case."

"What the hell?" I said out loud. I meant to say it in my head. But seeing the knife caught me off guard. It was the kind of knife that could cause a lot of damage. "You told me no one was going to get hurt."

"No one is, but you never know," Derick said. "You may need a little help."

"Where am I supposed to put it?" I asked.

I looked at Tay. His face said it all.

I held the handle.

And carefully slid the knife down the small of my back.

Chapter Seven

We walked to the shop in silence. The cold blade of the knife was a reminder of what was around the corner. I wanted to speak with Tay. But I didn't know what to say. What I needed to say was, *What the hell we doin', bro?! This was not part of the plan!!!*

But instead I said nothing.

No one spoke.

The five-minute walk felt like an hour. We rounded the corner to Mill Street. I checked my phone.

Eight forty. The shop would be closing soon. One good thing? It would be pretty much empty.

The streets were busy. Packed sidewalks. Laughter from strangers filled the air. But Mr. Yang's shop was in complete darkness. And Mr. Yang was getting into his car.

Derick was the first to speak. I don't know what he said. I do remember hearing a lot of cussing. Then it was Tay's turn.

"What time is it?" Tay asked.

I could see both of his hands were in tight fists. He looked like he was ready to fight.

I pulled my phone out my pocket. The knife blade felt like ice on my back. It took my attention away. But only for a moment. I was trying to focus my eyes on the numbers. Eight forty-seven. How could this be? Was my phone broken?

As we walked in front of Mr. Yang's car, he gave us the once-over.

"Closed," he said. "Broken lights." He didn't explain more. He just drove away.

We stood with our mouths open, watching Mr. Yang's car disappear.

I felt the sting in my jaw first. Then my right shoulder hitting the ground. The knife fell onto the ground. Dazed, I looked up. Tay was standing over me, screaming. Derick was trying his best to pull him off me.

"Yo, CHILL!" Derick shouted, getting between the two of us. "You lookin' to bring the cops to our front door?" He had both of his hands on Tay's chest.

People were looking. "If this guy hadn't fallen asleep, we'd be good!" Tay shouted. He was breathing heavy.

"And how is knocking him out gonna help us?" Derick asked.

"Okay, I get it," Tay said.

But I could tell he was still mad.

"Squash it now," Derick said again. But louder.

Tay put his hand out and helped me off the ground.

"Sorry, man," Tay said.

"It's all good," I said. But it wasn't. My jaw was throbbing, and I felt like my shoulder was dislocated.

But there was no way I was going to whine about it.

Derick looked at me. "You good, li'l man?" he asked.

He put his hand on my shoulder.

I groaned and pulled back. The pain shot through my whole body. "Yeah, I'm good."

Derick laughed. "You'll be fine. Nothing a good night's sleep won't take care of. Rest up, Jess. We're gonna need you in top form."

He went to hit me on my shoulder again. But I was too quick. I moved out of his way before he struck.

"Let's get out of here," Derick said. He was shoving the knife into the side pocket of his pants. I hadn't seen him pick it up. Guess I was too busy getting clocked.

I was in a lot of pain. But it wasn't my shoulder that was hurting, it was my ego. I'd thought Tay was my ride or die. My boy. I trusted him.

The walk back to the car was short. Tay went to get into the front seat. But Derick told him to get in the back.

Derick kept looking at me, like he wanted to make sure I was good. We pulled into my driveway. "Okay, kid," Derick said. "You sure you're good?"

"Yeah, I'm fine," I said.

"We'll pick you up on Friday, same time."

"Okay," I said.

Like I had a choice.

Now my shoulder was feeling it more than my ego. The pain was too much. I'm sure they could tell I wasn't fine. I opened the car door with my left hand.

"Here," Derick said, handing me the knife.

"I'm good," I said, shaking my head.

My shoulder was killing me.

"Nah, you hold onto it, kid," Derick said. "You can practice."

I took the knife from Derick. It took me a few seconds to get it behind my back. My arm wouldn't move right.

I turned around. "Later, Tay," I said.

"Later," Tay said, looking out the window. Then he jumped into the front seat and closed the door.

Derick drove off just as Grandpa pulled into the driveway. I wasn't even thinking about my shoulder. Or how I was going to explain it to him.

I was just happy he could unlock the door for me. The way my shoulder was throbbing, there was no way I was going to be able to do it.

Chapter Eight

My shoulder was sore all night. But the next day it felt a bit better. Grandpa asked me what happened. I told him I fell over playing soccer. I'm not sure he believed me. But since nothing was broken, I just iced it for a while. I relaxed all day Wednesday. Derick called to check on me. But Tay didn't call.

Thursday, neither of them called. I was relieved. Maybe this was over. I'd never get my new kicks, but at least no one would get hurt.

Friday morning rolled around. I still hadn't heard from Tay. Maybe I never would again. I'd never thought I would feel this way. Tay and I had been close for so long. *Ride or die.* Looked like that run was coming to an end.

"Jess?" I heard my grandpa call from downstairs.

I was glad. It took me out of my head. At least for a minute or two. I took the stairs, slowly this time. I had to steady myself on the landing. Not because of my shoulder. Because Tay was sitting at my kitchen table. I could not hide the look on my face.

My grandpa looked at me and then at Tay.

"I have some things to do," Grandpa said. "I'll leave you boys alone."

We watched him leave.

"You good?" Tay asked me a second later.

"You tell me," I said.

I was angry but cool enough to keep my voice low. I didn't want Grandpa to hear us.

Tay said, "Just hear me out, please."

Something had happened. Something had shifted. Tay wasn't angry anymore.

He looked confused.

Tay was one of those kids. His gear matched his personality. Cool gear for a cool kid. But that was not the kid in front of me. I had known Tay for years. Something was up. His head dropped.

"What's going on, Tay?" I asked. "We're best friends. You can tell me anything. Talk to me."

Tay did. He talked to me. He told me the reason why he was going through with the plan. He told me *everything.*

Turned out Derick was a fraud. He preyed on younger kids. Got them to believe he wanted to be friends. That was what had happened to Tay last summer. He met Derick when he was on vacation with his family. At the mall. Tay was hanging out with his cousin. Derick came up to them, started chatting.

"He lures kids into his fancy lifestyle," Tay said. "Makes you believe you're his boy. Gains your trust, then gets you to hit up stores."

Same thing we were planning for Mr. Yang's place.

Tay went on. "Then Derick holds it over their heads. Gets them to do a few more. If they refuse, he says he'll go to the police."

That didn't make sense to me.

"If Derick went to the police, he could get himself in trouble too," I said.

"Derick doesn't do the dirty work," Tay explained. "He preps the boys and secretly records them going over the plan. If we don't go through with it, he threatens to release the recording. And that's how he makes his money."

"Through his foot soldiers." I sighed.

"I heard he's also dealing drugs," Tay said.

I don't doubt it, I thought. That would explain all of Derick's dope swag.

Tay told me Derick had a voice recording and video of him admitting to another robbery.

"I'm sorry, man," Tay said. "Derick said he would erase the recordings from his phone if I got you involved." I could hear it in his voice. He was trying to hold in the tears. He was embarrassed.

I didn't know if I should be angry at Tay for throwing me under the bus. Or angry at Derick for being such a jerk. Either way Derick had to go. And there was only one way.

We'd have to go through with it. I'd just have to be real careful. Careful about what

I said to Derick. Then, once we were done, it would be over.

"Listen," I said. "We have a plan. Let's stick to the plan. Maybe if I give Derick a bigger cut, he'll leave you alone. Leave us both alone."

"Once he gets hold of you, he doesn't let go," Tay said.

"Lemme ask you something," I said. "Why did you punch me? Why were you so angry at me?"

Tay sighed. His head dropped again. "It wasn't you I was angry at," he said. "That night I finally saw a way out! I figured he'd leave me alone. I know. It's crazy. It's been going on for so long. I didn't know what to do. I should have told you. I was afraid you'd drop me."

"Look," I said. "You've been my ride or die since third grade. You were there for me when my folks died. I'm not going to let this clown destroy that. You said he loves the money. So let's give him what he loves. Play it cool. Don't let Derick think anything has changed. Let him think we're good."

Tay raised his head.

I grabbed his hand. "We can do this," I said.

Chapter Nine

Friday night it was hot. We parked in the same place. But we got there forty-five minutes before Mr. Yang's shop closed. Derick was going to "run" this one with us. Lucky us—looked like we were the chosen ones. Derick had wanted to go through everything over the phone. I'd insisted we do it in person.

As we sat in the car, Derick began to go over the plan. It had changed. I had messed up the first time. So this time I was going to grab the cash from Yang's register. He repeated everything, like he thought Tay and I were stupid.

My mind started to drift. But I knew this wasn't the time to be in my head.

I heard my dad's voice. *Stay in the game, son.*

"Yo, can I use your phone?" I asked Derick. "I need to text my grandpa."

"What happened to yours?" Derick asked.

"It's dead," I said.

"What about your boy's?" Derick said, looking at Tay.

"I forgot mine at home," Tay said.

Derick laughed. "That's why I don't like dealing with kids. They never come ready to take care of business." He handed me his phone. "Make it quick. We're about to roll."

Derick started bragging to Tay about his house. About how he got all his money and his cool clothes. About how he got boys to work for him. And how great he thought he was. God, he loved himself. His voice was making me sick. I couldn't wait to get this over with.

"Why so shifty, bro?" Derick asked. "Scared?"

"No, the knife is sticking me in my leg," I said.

"At least someone came ready to do business," Derick said, looking back at Tay.

I hoped Derick wasn't trying to be my best friend. That spot was taken. I handed Derick back his phone.

At eight forty we walked to the shop in silence.

Tonight there was no one on the streets. When we got to Mr. Yang's, there were three people in the store. Derick was super hyped.

"Look, I'll do this, but I'm not carrying the knife," I said.

"Doesn't matter," Derick said. "This is going to be like taking candy from a kid. Give me the knife."

I handed it over, and Derick shoved it in his pocket.

I looked at Tay. He nodded. Derick walked into the store first. A minute or two later Tay followed. I was the last to go in.

The last customer was just leaving. Derick walked over to the chip aisle. Tay headed for the cooler with the drinks. Yang looked up. As predicted, he came out from behind the register and walked toward the boys.

Too bad Yang didn't know who the real threat was.

I knew Tay would keep Yang busy. But with three of us in the store, Yang would have to pick and choose. I walked toward the counter. Derick had said there would be a good amount of money. It had been hot that day.

Tay did a good job of keeping Yang busy.

I made my way toward the register. Yang turned. All of a sudden he was looking at me. Derick saw this and jumped into action.

He started making noise. Talking real loud, laughing and carrying on. Yang shouted at Derick.

"I'm closing soon," Yang said. He was annoyed. "Hurry up! Get what you need and get going."

All the kids in the area were used to Yang's treatment. But for some reason, Derick thought he was special. He didn't like how Yang was speaking to him. Derick began to get loud, rude. Shouting and swearing at Yang. Yang was old, but he was bold. He stepped up to Derick and began to yell back. Louder than

Derick. Yang wasn't afraid. He took his finger and pushed it into Derick's chest.

Derick lost his cool. He pushed Yang so hard that he landed on the floor, hitting his face on the bottom shelf. Then Derick swept his arm over the chip rack. Bags of chips flew everywhere. Yang looked stunned, but he was still in the fight. Derick reached into his pocket and pulled out the knife.

"You messin' with me, old man?" I heard Derick say as he pointed the blade of the knife toward Yang.

Yang's eyes widened. He began to speak in Korean. I don't know if he was angry or scared. But I had seen enough. I needed to stop this.

"Yo, man, leave him alone!" I yelled. "Get out of here!"

Derick ran out of the store, Tay on his heels. I followed. I don't know if we were all just scared or confused, but we ended up running the wrong way. In the opposite direction of where Derick's car was parked.

After what seemed like forever, we stopped running. Derick was laughing. Tay looked just as dazed as I felt. Then all of a sudden Derick stopped laughing.

He looked at me. Something in his eyes said he wasn't playing. But he was the one who was about to get played.

"How much you take the old man for?" he asked. He began to walk toward me. He was real close to me. In my face. Nose to nose.

"Nothing," I said. I was so close to Derick, I could smell his breath. When you're that close to someone, you can feel their next move. Derick's came quick. He grabbed me by my shirt.

"You think I'm playing?" Derick said. "Your boy is going down."

"I don't think so," I said.

Derick pulled me closer to him. "What'd you say to me?"

I pushed him off me. Reaching into my pocket, I took out my phone. I opened it to my recordings and pressed *play*.

I watched the blood drain from Derick's face. He stood silent, listening to the voice recording of all the crap he'd said in the car. The whole plan. And all his bragging.

"Because you're such a waste of space, man, I've got more for you," I said with a grin on my face.

I showed Derick the video recording of his two-minute assault on Mr. Yang. I'd had my phone in my hand the whole time.

"You're not going to say anything about Tay," I said. "I deleted all the recordings from your phone. Maybe you have a backup. But so what? If that gets out, so does your beat-down on Mr. Yang."

I looked at Tay. "Let's go." We turned toward the shop.

Mr. Yang probably didn't know who Derick was. So he might not tie us to the assault.

But there was no way we could live with ourselves if we didn't go back and help him.

I know you're scared, son.

I know you'll do the right thing.

So that's what I decided to do. I had no idea how Mr. Yang would react. But I knew I couldn't do nothing.

I was so in my head, I didn't even know Derick was still standing there.

He was flapping his mouth. Something about how soft we were. And how he knew he couldn't ask boys to do a man's job.

"Trust me..." Derick started to say. I walked over to him.

I'd said I was going to punch the next person who said "Trust me." Derick happened to be the lucky winner. I balled up my fist and planted a right hook on his left check. Derick stumbled back a few steps. He lost his balance and fell hard on the pavement.

My knuckles were red. They burned. It was the best feeling.

The air felt cooler. For the first time in days, I felt calm.

"Let's get outta here, Tay," I said.

Tay looked surprised. He also looked relieved. He was probably wanting to knock Derick out too.

When we got to the shop, we were surprised to find the door unlocked. It was close to closing. And after the beatdown Mr. Yang had taken, he was in no condition to serve any customers.

We opened the door. We saw that some of the chips had been cleaned up. But for the most part, the store looked exactly the same.

We heard a woman's voice at the front of the store.

"Sorry, boys, the store is closed."

We looked up and saw a tall dark-skinned woman standing in front of Mr. Yang.

She was wearing a suit and had a notepad in her hands.

"What happened?" I asked.

I knew full well what had happened.

"Mr. Yang was assaulted tonight. I'm Detective Baker," she said.

I felt the blood begin to drain from my face.

Cops and Black boys are never a good combination.

Mr. Yang looked up.

He was sitting on a stool, holding an ice pack to his right cheek. He looked like someone who had lost everything. Not money. But something bigger.

His pride.

Mr. Yang's eyes widened as he pointed at me and Tay.

"They were here," he said. "They saw everything."

The detective looked at us. By the look on her face, I could tell she knew something was up.

"Boys, is that true?" she asked. "Were you here?"

I stared at her. I didn't trust cops. That was the message that had been drilled into me since I was a kid. But this time I wasn't afraid. It was different. I heard my dad's voice.

Sometimes, son, you need to do what scares you most.

It was like I could see him standing behind the cop, wearing his favorite kicks.

I will always be by your side.

I looked over at Tay. He had been my boy for years. I knew what that look meant.

"We'd like to call home first," I said.

Reaching slowly into my pocket, I pulled out my phone.

My dad's voice was just a whisper in my head now. But he was there.

I love you, Jesse.

ORCA ANCHOR

FIND YOUR

Jen learns that her mom has been keeping a secret: Jen has a biological father who isn't the dad she grew up with. Now this secret threatens to tear their family apart.

"BOTH A COMING-OF-AGE STORY AND A ROAD MAP FOR PROCESSING DIFFICULT EMOTIONS."

—Kirkus Reviews

Dex is dropped onto a deserted tropical island to compete in an internet reality show. He will do whatever it takes to gain the most likes and social media followers needed to win. But is is worth it?

"A COMPACT, EXISTENTIAL, REALITY-SHOW ADVENTURE WITH STRONG RELUCTANT READER APPEAL."

—Kirkus Reviews

NEXT READ!

Kai is angry when he's forced to join his new stepdad on a research trip to Blind Bay. But when an ancient predator awakens, they need to work together to stop the creature before it's too late.

"ENGAGING AND HOOKS READERS FROM START TO FINISH."
—School Library Journal

After a massive earthquake hits, Amy and her estranged half sister, Mara, journey through the aftermath in search of their parents. What will they find in the wreckage?

"AN INTRIGUING PREMISE...[WITH] NONSTOP ACTION."
—Kirkus Reviews

Julie Thompson is the author of the picture book *When Isaac Hears the Rain*. She creates stories that celebrate the lived experiences of children everywhere. As a mother of two boys, she is especially drawn to books that honor Black Boy joy. Julie's stories are inspired by the people, places and experiences that have shaped her world. When she's not writing, you can find Julie on her yoga mat, spending time in nature or hitting the pavement, clocking miles as she explores the streets of Toronto.